Imagine this...You're about to cross the mile marker as you approach the end of mile three. There is only one-tenth of a mile to go! Your heart is pounding even more rapidly than it was before as you hear the rapidly approaching shrill of the enthusiastic crowd cheering on the finishers.

Your legs feel like Jell-O and you begin to question your internal strength. *"Can I make it to the end, or will I crumble to the ground? I need to stop. I can't do it! Wait, what am I saying?"* you ask yourself. *"I'm doing great; can't stop now! Yes, you can!"* You pick up your pace and enter a new level of speed and strength with every step.

Now imagine this...An innocent nine-year-old girl with a disease or dystrophy making it impossible for her to ever walk or run. She is sitting in a jogging chair, while you have been trusted to be her feet, so you run; you run like the wind!

Can you envision this? Well, I certainly can because I have done that on many occasions. You see, my younger sister, Ainsley, is that amazing little girl in the running chair and I am her legs! Running is something that has become very special to me because I am able to connect with Ainsley like never before. I see the huge smile on her face and it tells me that she loves it, too. Perhaps you should start running, and who knows, maybe one day you will run with the wind, too!

Born an Angel

For Ainsley; my sister, my friend, my inspiration.

written by: Briley Rossiter

illustrated by: Jennifer Carlson Ware

All author proceeds from the sale of *Born an Angel* are pledged
by Briley to the Ainsley's Angels of America Foundation.
www.AinsleysAngels.org

When I found out that I was going to have a little sister joining our family of three, I was afraid. Before she was born, I was the only child and never left my mom's side. Being her only child, I was her favorite child and did not want to share her with anyone.

I was only two years old when my baby sister was born. We named her Ainsley. Once I saw her and how tiny and innocent she was I did not mind sharing Mom with her. Ainsley was absolutely beautiful. Who would have ever guessed on the cold December night when Ainsley entered our world that my life would change forever?

For years, Mom had dreamed of having two little girls. They would play dress-up, have tea parties, and play with dolls for hours on end. Mom would get to experience her very own little princesses, laughing, running around the house, and growing together. She would make us tea and cut toast in little triangles, while we imagined life as members of the Royal Family. Mom's dream only lasted for a little while, as by Ainsley's second birthday, she still wasn't walking. My mom, dad, and I knew that something wasn't right.

We brought Ainsley to the hospital and she had test after test and therapy upon therapy. Nobody knew what was wrong. I was really scared and realized that I was still afraid like I was before Ainsley was born, but now in a different way. The sister I didn't think I wanted to begin with, I now knew I didn't want to be without. It's sort of funny how things change as time passes.

After months of testing, we finally found a doctor who knew what was wrong with Ainsley. He was a neurologist and had only heard of one other case like it in all his years of medicine. He explained that Ainsley is only one of a few people in the United States with a disease called Infantile Neuroaxonal Dystrophy (INAD), an illness as ugly as it sounds. INAD is an extremely rare genetic disorder that causes Ainsley's nerves to slowly stop working. The doctor told us that she has a life expectancy of only five to ten years.

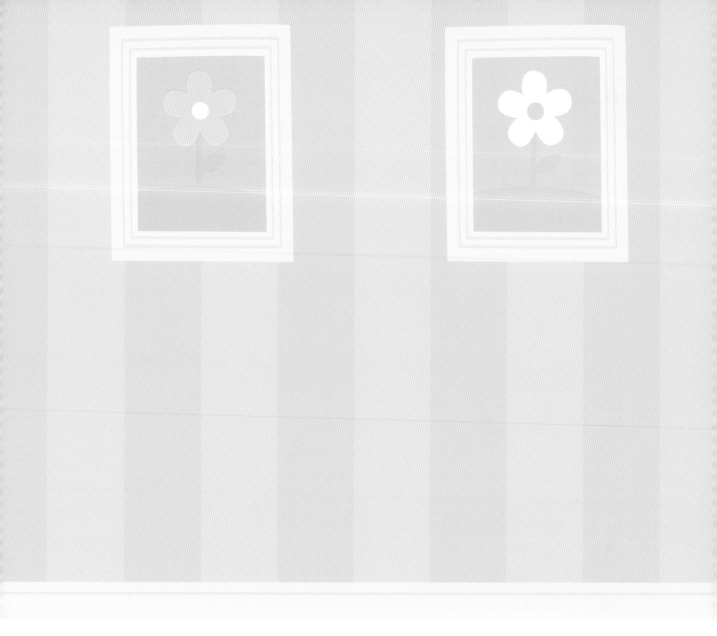

As quickly as my life changed when Ainsley entered my world, now it changed again. Ainsley is different than I am but she is still my sister. Ainsley rides in a wheelchair and is unable to walk and talk. She doesn't play for fun and cannot laugh with her friends. Ainsley isn't able to go to school, but has a teacher that comes to our house once a week to read and do crafts with her. She can no longer eat through her mouth, so Mom and Dad feed her using a special tube that goes right into her stomach. Our goal is to make Ainsley's life as memorable as possible for her and to make sure she enjoys every moment.

One day, Ainsley's physical therapist introduced our family to a local running group that participated in road races. The group was called Team Hoyt Virginia Beach and was inspired by Massachusetts native, father-son team, Dick and Rick Hoyt. The Hoyt's have become world-famous because Rick has spent his entire life in a wheelchair and Dick pushes him in races from start to finish. They have competed in over one thousand races. The physical therapist told us that Team Hoyt Virginia Beach wanted to create athletic events that disabled children and adults can compete in and enjoy with able-bodied participants.

Their goal was to create events such as 5Ks, 10Ks, half-marathons, and triathlons. These disabled athletes are pushed and pulled over the land and through the water using special equipment. We learned that the disabled athlete is referred to as the Captain, while the pusher is known as the Angel. She gave us their website address and the date of their next race. Our whole family left the physical therapist's office with huge smiles on our faces and a warm feeling in our hearts. Mom would finally get to see her little princesses playing together as she once imagined.

After watching my sister participate as a Captain with so many other disabled children and adults and watching them being pushed by Angels, including our own dad, I became inspired to run, too. Running was something that no one thought Ainsley would ever be able to enjoy, let alone something we would enjoy together. After sitting on the sidelines for her entire life, Ainsley was finally able to go; to run; to roll with the wind!

I began running alongside my dad and Ainsley nearly every weekend and became the youngest Angel on Team Hoyt Virginia Beach. I quickly learned that running in races was fun, but it was also a lot of work and could be extremely nerve-racking. Ainsley and I would stand with the other competitors, waiting for the starter's gun to go off. I could feel my heart begin to race before we even rolled across the starting line. I know that Ainsley's heart was beating fast, too.

I would often find myself at the starting line with Ainsley, waiting for my race, our race, to begin. Imagine this: *I'm stretched and hydrated. "FIVE," booms the voice of the race director behind the microphone. My shoelaces are tied into two tight knots. "FOUR." My race bib is securely fastened to my shirt. "THREE." The restless crowd falls silent. "TWO." I order myself to calm down as I take one final deep breath. "ONE." I bend over the jogging chair ready to strike, "ERRRRRRRR!" the horn blows, signaling the start. "Let's do this, Ains!" I yell to Ainsley over the roar of the crowd. And off we go.*

Since Ainsley and I ran our first race, together we have participated in nearly a dozen races. Ainsley and my dad have done nearly forty races of varying lengths, from 5Ks, 8Ks, and 10Ks, to half-marathons. They even completed the Marine Corps Full Marathon together in Washington DC, which is an amazing 26.2 miles long. Ainsley and I even competed in a 5K alongside Dick and Rick Hoyt, themselves. Dad says watching us cross the finish line in step with the Hoyts was one of the highlights of his life. I think Ainsley probably feels the same way. Crossing the finish line in step with the legends that made all of this possible, was a memory to behold.

Nearly everything that I have been able to do in my entire life, Ainsley cannot do. Ainsley can't walk or talk or laugh. She can't jump or play with dolls, ride a bike or chase butterflies. She can't even truly participate in the tea party that Mom envisioned for so long. But there is one thing that Ainsley is able to do better than anyone I have ever met; one thing that I could never begin to do without her and one thing that she certainly does even better than me. Ainsley inspires. Ainsley has inspired thousands of people all over the country.

You can't meet Ainsley without being inspired and you always leave with
a smile on your face, that familiar lump in your throat, and warmth in your
heart. Recently, the legend of Ainsley grew even larger and wider as she
inspired yet another person, our aunt. Like everyone else that Ainsley meets,
our aunt was inspired to do something amazing. After watching all of the fun
that we were having running with Ainsley in Virginia, she started running and
spreading Ainsley's inspiration in Louisiana, where our family roots remain.

After experiencing the joy of pushing Ainsley in a race, our aunt and Ainsley's former pre-school teacher in North Carolina joined with Dad and several others to create two running groups similar to Team Hoyt Virginia Beach. They are called myTEAM Triumph-Ainsley's Angels of Southwest Louisiana and myTEAM Triumph-Ainsley's Angels of Eastern Carolina. These two groups are among fifteen other myTEAM chapters across the United States.

Ainsley has inspired many others, from
family and friends to neighbors and
doctors. She inspires nearly everyone who
has the pleasure to meet her. It's hard to imagine that one day our
Ainsley will be gone; a day closer to us than I choose to think about.
But as I sit and think about all the people that she has touched, I
realize that Ainsley will leave behind a beautiful thing; a legacy that
will live on forever. Love you, Angel.

Glossary of Terms

5k: A 5k race (Five kilometers) is equal to 3.1 miles

8k: An 8k race (Eight kilometers) is equal to 4.9 miles

10k: A 10k race (Ten kilometers) is equal to 6.2 miles

Competitors: Someone who competes

Half-Marathon: A 13.1 mile race

Inspire: To influence someone in a good way

Legacy: A thing or idea passed along from one person to another

Marathon: A 26.2 mile race

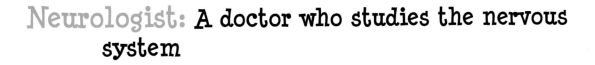

Neurologist: A doctor who studies the nervous system

Physical Therapist: Someone who provides treatment of a disorder (massage, exercise, and heat)

Triathlon: A race which includes running, biking, and swimming

Briley and Ainsley Rossiter

About the Author

Briley Rossiter lives in Virginia Beach, Virginia, with her parents, brother, and sister, Ainsley. She and her family have been members of a local running group, Team Hoyt Virginia Beach, since summer of 2008. Briley is a sixth grader enrolled in the Middle Years International Baccalaureate World School program. She enjoyed writing this book about her relationship with her sister and dreams that it will one day be in every elementary school in America. She is considering writing a second book in the future and enjoys listening to music, spending time with her friends, traveling, and running.

About the Illustrator

Jennifer Ware lives in The Woodlands, Texas, with her husband and three children. She owns Zenware Designs, an illustration and design company, started in 2004 so that she could stay at home with her little ones. She is honored to take part in Briley's dream.